Hazel the Guinea Pig

A. N. Wilson has written over twenty stories for grown-ups, many of which have won prizes such as the Somerset Maugham Award (for *The Healing Art)* and the 1988 Whitbread Award (for the biography *Tolstoy*). He has also written the story of the exciting adventures of a hamster in a book called *Furball and the Mokes* and the tale of an old cat looking back over his life, called *Stray*. He has had many pets in his life, including dogs and cats. His three daughters have, between them, had rabbits, guinea pigs, hamsters, goldfish and dogs.

Also by A. N. Wilson

Furball and the Mokes

Hazel
the Guinea Pig

A.N. WILSON

CORVUS

First published in Great Britain in 1989 by Walker Books Ltd.

Published in paperback in Great Britain in 2012 by Corvus, an imprint
of Atlantic Books Ltd.

10 9 8 7 6 5 4 3 2 1

A CIP catalogue record for this book is available
from the British Library.

Paperback ISBN: 978 0 85789 078 8
E-book ISBN: 978 0 85789 079 5

Printed in Italy by 🦌 Grafica Veneta SpA

Corvus
An imprint of Atlantic Books Ltd
Ormond House
26–27 Boswell Street |
London
WC1N 3JZ

www.corvus-books.co.uk

Contents

Hazel's Search

Hazel was a brown, sleek, beautiful guinea pig with eyes as glossy and black as raisins. Like most guinea pigs, Hazel enjoyed her food. She was far from slender. To be honest, Hazel was a very fat guinea pig indeed. In fact, she was so fat that she looked as though she had been blown up like a balloon. Her cheeks bulged. Her black-curranty eyes seemed to pop out of her ample face. And her body was a sphere, a pudding of glossy brown fur.

But Hazel was an extremely handsome creature. It suited her to be fat, just as it suits some *people* to be fat. And fat is what she was.

*Hazel was a brown, sleek, beautiful guinea pig
with eyes as glossy and black as raisins.*

Hazel liked to explore. When she was in her hutch, she sometimes ran from one room to the next, as though she were looking for something. Life in two rooms becomes more interesting if it can be turned into an everlasting quest. She waddled into her living room and ate some food. Then she nuzzled about behind the food bowl, as if she were looking for something there. Then she ran back into her bedroom and burrowed into the hay, as though she had lost something – something very precious.

When her young owner got her out of the hutch, Hazel liked to explore some more.

'No,' she seemed to say, turning this way and that on someone's lap. 'It's not here. Let's try up there.' And she would scuttle up under someone's jersey.

'Hazel loves going up your jumper,' said one of the children, one afternoon when their mother was out at the shops.

'Yes, she does,' agreed the other child. 'She likes to explore.'

'I suppose I do,' thought Hazel. 'I like to explore. I wonder what there is down *this* dark passage. I'll just have a look. You never know.'

When she went down that dark passage, Hazel felt wool pressing hard against her cheeks, and she heard the girl's voice crying out, 'Hazel! What are you doing?'

'She is going up your jumper,' said the boy's voice.

Hazel tried to advance further into the sleeve-tunnel, but it was tight and dark and woolly. Before long, she could feel the girl pulling at her hind legs and dragging her back into the daylight.

Hazel wriggled and struggled to be free. She had begun to feel a bit peckish, and she would not have refused if someone had offered her a piece of brown bread or a carrot. (These were her favourite foods.)

She found that the girl had put her down on the kitchen floor, and she was able to run about freely. Here there was much to explore.

'Worth a look,' thought Hazel, as she scuttled to the other end of the kitchen and peered between the bars of a fender. A fire was glowing beyond the bars, and Hazel wondered whether she might have a closer look at it. Very bright, fire is. Very interesting. On the other hand, it is also… Hazel wondered how she would describe it. Well, hot would be one word. The bars of the fender almost hurt her nose before she had started to sniff them.

'I remember now,' she thought. 'Fire's hot. Ar well, now that I've had a look at that, it is time to search about for… for…'

What was it that Hazel was always searching for and seeking?

She ran along the skirting board and listened at a mousehole. All was quiet within, for this usehold with cats. There was no mouse merrymaking there.

Hazel peered at the bottom of a cupboard. But the door was shut.

And then, at the other end of the kitchen, she saw another door. This time, it was an open door.

No one was taking as much notice of her as they should have done when Hazel, very swift, though very fat on her short legs, made her rapid progress towards the open door. She ran! Oh, how Hazel ran! She ran out of the kitchen and into the tiled hall, through the legs of a chair, and up to a most interesting selection of articles lying higgledy-piggledy by the back door.

'Now,' Hazel asked herself, 'what have we here?'

She had stopped feeling slightly peckish. She had become extremely hungry. And she had decided that there was no point in waiting for someone to give her a stalk or a leaf, a carrot or a crust. She should go and look for them. That's what she would do.

Hazel's mind had wandered a bit by the time she reached the heap of interesting articles. She had forgotten, exactly, what it was that she had decided. Explore, that would be it. But what for?

Now then, what had she here? Hazel paused. In that moment, she looked as round and as brown and as sleek and as fat as she had ever looked in her life. Just ahead of her nose, she had seen a Wellington boot resting on its side.

'Well,' said Hazel to herself, 'if that isn't a tunnel! What was it that I had decided to go and do? *Explore*! That was it. Well, where better to explore than up a tunnel? And – me being hungry and all, who knows? Like as not, there's a carrot or a bit of brown bread at the end of that … yes, that tunnel. Tunnel's the word for it.'

In short, Hazel was stuck.

And with great eagerness, Hazel advanced into the Wellington boot. Inside it smelt rather rubbery, but she pressed on, fearless, towards the toe.

'Now this,' she thought, 'is what I'd call dark. Very, very dark, this tunnel. Dark and – ' she added to herself as she got further and further inside the boot – 'dark and, well, narrow would be one word for it. Yes, I would definitely say that this tunnel was narrow. Still, what was it? Carrots and crusts?'

By now Hazel was in complete darkness, and she realised two very disagreeable facts. One was that the sides of the tunnel were narrower than her own fat little body. Another sad fact was that, though her feet were still scampering and scuttling, she had stopped moving.

In short, Hazel was stuck.

She had never walked backwards in her life. She had only walked forwards. And the more she scampered and scuttled with her sharp little claws, the more stuck Hazel became. The sides of the Wellington boot pressed against her fur. She had become a prisoner.

⁂

In the kitchen, the children had noticed Hazel's absence, but they were unable to explain it.

'Hazel!' called the girl's voice. 'Hazel, where are you?'

'You should have looked where she was going,' said the boy's voice.

'It wasn't my fault,' said the girl, whose voice had become a little quavery. 'Hazel! Hazel, darling! Where *are* you?'

The little girl, who was nearly eight (tomorrow would be her birthday), had begun a frantic search for her beloved guinea pig at one end of the kitchen. Her elder brother, aged ten, sat and watched.

The girl looked behind the fender. Hazel could surely not have got into the fire? She looked at the mousehole in the skirtingboard. Hazel could surely not have got through that! She looked behind the sofa. She even looked in the cupboard. But Hazel was nowhere to be seen.

'I expect she fell in the fire,' said the boy unpleasantly. 'She's probably burnt up by now. Mum shouldn't let you keep a guinea pig if you can't look after it.'

'What about your hamster, then?'

'That was different, and besides, I was only six. I looked *after* Hammy. It wasn't my fault he escaped. You can't look after Hazel.'

'I can.'

'Why are you crying, then?'

'I'm not…' *crying*, his sister tried to say. But by the end of her sentence, she was.

Hazel did not have an opinion about whether the girl was crying. She only wished that they could get her out of the tunnel. She let out agonised squeaks to inform the children of her predicament.

The little girl, through her sobs, came out into the hall and heard Hazel squeaking. But she could not tell where Hazel was hidden.

'Hazel!' she called again. 'Where are you?'

But what could a guinea pig *do*? She could not say the words: 'I am in a tunnel. Stuck would be the word for it.' She could only squeal, and when this had no effect she was once more silent.

'I heard her. I really heard her out here,' said the girl.

'You're making such a noise yourself, how could you hear her?' her brother asked crossly.

'She was squealing,' said the girl.

'I can't see her,' said the boy.

Hazel heard him kick the hall chair and scrape its legs on the tiles. The children were looking underneath the chair. Then they opened the cupboard under the stairs and called Hazel's name.

They had no idea that she was just under their noses, stuck in the Wellington boot.

Inside the boot it was still very dark. It also felt hot and Hazel was beginning to find it difficult to breathe. There was another strange thing. The longer she stayed in the narrow tunnel, the narrower it seemed. She felt the sides of the boot grow tighter and tighter against her sides. Surely she was not actually getting fatter inside the boot? By now she was ravenously hungry, and she could not remember when she last saw a decent cabbage stalk or a bowl of bran. It was a sorry state that Hazel had got herself into, and the thought of it made her start squealing again. This time she was not squealing to alert the children. She was just squealing in despair.

'I heard her that time,' said the boy. 'I suppose she hasn't got underneath that pile of boots and shoes by the back door?'

No sooner had these words been spoken than Hazel felt the tunnel heaving and shaking and shuddering.

Thump!

Something had fallen on top of the tunnel.

Bang!

To the right and left of her, boots, shoes, roller-skates, trainers, tennis balls, and rubber flip-flops were being thrown.

And then Hazel got the feeling you get in a fairground if ever you are brave and silly enough to go on the roller coaster. Her stomach heaved and jumped. And although she was still squeezed tight in the blackness of the tunnel, she felt the tunnel being lifted into the air.

'She's in the Wellington boot!' the boy cried aloud from the back door.

'Where? Where? Give her to me!' shouted his sister.

'Don't be rough.'

'I'm not being rough.'

'You are.'

'Give her to me,' said the girl crossly.

While these words were being exchanged, Hazel could feel the tunnel swaying about in the air and being dragged to and fro. And then she heard the girl say, 'We'll put you on the kitchen table, Hazel dear, and we shall have you out in a jiffy.'

'A jiffy, eh?' thought Hazel. 'Well, I'd rather be in a jiffy than in a tunnel. Just as long as it isn't what I would call a *narrow* jiffy.'

But before she had time to ask herself what a jiffy *was*, Hazel was screaming with violent agony and terror. The girl's hand had reached inside the Wellington boot and was pulling Hazel by her hind legs. It felt as if she were having her legs pulled off. However much the girl pulled at the back, the front part of Hazel's body still remained stuck in the boot. And the more the girl pulled, the more Hazel screamed and the more she wanted to get away from the pain by burrowing deeper and deeper into the toe of the boot.

'You're hurting her,' said the boy.

'I'm trying to get her out. Come on, Hazel.'

And once more, the girl thrust her hand into the boot in an attempt to extricate the captive.

But Hazel was stuck. She was more stuck than ever. And by now her screams could have been heard half a mile away. She sounded like a big farmyard pig just about to be made into bacon.

'Let's have a go,' said the boy.

But the boy's hand was bigger than his sister's, and he was afraid to get hold of Hazel lest he squash her altogether. He tried, as gently as he could, to hold the boot upside down and to shake Hazel out. Her screams did not grow any quieter.

'There is only one thing to do,' said the girl. 'We will have to cut the boot with some scissors, the way some babies are born.'

'Mum will go spare if you cut my boot,' said the boy.

'But Hazel is *stuck*,' said the girl.

Hazel, very much stuck, stopped screaming for a moment and listened. She heard one of the children opening a drawer. She heard the rattle of metal objects. Then the boot began to heave and to shake once more, and the children were once more quarrelling.

'It's my boot.'

'She's my guinea pig.'

'You'll jab her if you wave those scissors like that.'

'I forbid you to cut my boot.'

'Hard cheese.'

'Either you give me those scissors and let me

Either you give me those scissors and let me cut the boot,
or Hazel will stay in the boot and die.

cut the boot, or Hazel will stay in the boot and die. Oh, stop *blubbering.*'

Hazel was silent. She was dumb with terror. The tunnel had started to shake again, and at her back she could hear the noise of scissor blades, coming closer and closer and closer. Snip! Snip! Snip!

'I'll have to cut the boot all the way up.'

'Well, mind you don't cut Hazel.'

'I'll feel it when the scissors go anywhere near her body,' said the boy.

'You mean, *she'll* feel it,' said the girl.

Hazel could indeed feel it. She could feel the cold steel of the blade creeping up the hot fat side of her body. And as soon as the scissors touched her, she screamed again.

'You've stabbed her!'

'Cripes!'

'You've stabbed her!'

'Of course I haven't.'

But the boy did not sound very sure. His scissors *had* come very close to the guinea pig, and he could not be sure whether or not he had accidentally nicked her with the blade.

But, in fact, Hazel was all right. Suddenly she saw daylight. The walls of the tunnel were ripped away. A hand was clasping her firmly and gently and giving her to the girl.

'Here you are. No cuts. She's quite safe.'

What a relief! What a drama!

In a few minutes Hazel found herself sitting on the girl's lap nibbling a cauliflower stalk. It was very consoling to be free again, and I am sorry to say that in the excitement of the moment, Hazel also made a rather large puddle over the girl's dress.

'Never mind, Hazel. This is not the dress which I am wearing to my birthday party tomorrow. Do you know what Mum is giving me for my birthday, Hazel? She says it's a surprise. But now that you are safe and well, I can't imagine a nicer present than you, dear Hazel; just you, safe and well again after your adventure.'

Well, an adventure was one thing you could call it. Hazel was not sure, but she thought you could easily call it an adventure. As for birthday presents, she did not know about those. At the moment, she was finding the cauliflower stalk most sustaining. When she had eaten enough, she burrowed once more into the girl's jumper. Now, what *was* it she had been looking for when she first set out to explore and got stuck in that horrible tunnel?

Coming back into the kitchen a few minutes later, the boy said, 'I've put the boot in an old plastic bag and hidden it in the dustbin. The dustbin men come tomorrow.'

'And tomorrow is my birthday!' said his sister. She was happy now. All her tears were dry.

'I don't know what I'm supposed to wear when it next rains,' said the boy. 'But it is true that those boots were getting tight for me and one of them leaked. Mum keeps saying she'll get me some new ones, but she never remembers.'

Just then they heard the squawk and squeak of their mother's bicycle brakes. Looking through the window, the boy saw his mother leaning her bicycle against the far wall at the end of the garden and hurrying into the shed where Hazel's hutch was kept.

'Mum's back,' said the boy. 'Here she is, coming down the garden path. And it looks as though she has a parcel for your birthday.'

'Is that my birthday present, Mum?' asked the girl when their mother came indoors and placed a large bag on the kitchen table.

'Your birthday present is a surprise,' said Mum. 'This bag is some more boots for your brother. He said that the old ones fit, but they were getting tight.' And out of her bag she produced a lovely pair of black, shiny Wellington boots, as black and shiny as Hazel's eyes.

'Thanks, Mum,' said the boy. 'You're right, my old boots were getting a bit tight.'

'They shouldn't leave them lying about,' Hazel thought. 'Not if they are tight, and a girl might feel inclined to go exploring up them. No wonder I got stuck, if they were tight. Tight is what they felt.'

The new boots, apparently, were a perfect fit. While the boy tried them on and expressed his pleasure in them, Mum talked to Hazel and the girl.

'Here you sit, Hazel,' said Mum, 'and I have been cycling around town, buying boots and I don't know what. You have a lucky life.'

'Well,' said the girl, but her brother shot her a glance that made it clear that she should not

'Oh, look what she's done on your dress!'

tell Mum the story of how Hazel got stuck in the boot, and how they had to cut her out of it with kitchen scissors.

'Is it a dull life for you, Hazel?' asked Mum, stroking the back of the guinea pig's head. 'All on your own, with nothing to do?'

'I don't think it's dull,' said the girl.

'I think it's a *bit* dull,' said Mum. 'You can't really imagine a guinea pig having an adventure, can you? She just has her food, and she scampers about and… oh, look what she's done on your dress! Come on Hazel, back in the hutch before you do any more damage.'

'My dress is drying now,' said the girl.

'I'll put her back in the hutch just the same,' said Mum.

'I will,' said the girl.

'No,' said Mum, 'you stay here. I will put Hazel back in the hutch.'

Mum went to the larder and came back with two carrots and two lumps of bread.

'Mum!' said the girl. 'Hazel's fat enough as it is. She'll burst if she eats all that.'

'She might get hungry,' said Mum.

'Quite right,' thought Hazel. 'You never know when you might get what I call hungry.'

'Come on, Hazel,' said Mum. And Hazel, who by now had recovered from the secret adventure of the boot, was very happy when Mum picked her up and carried her off down the garden path.

Mum opened the door of the hutch very carefully with one hand and put inside it the two carrots and the two lumps of bread.

'Carrots,' thought Hazel. 'Now I must remember to look for those. I'll have a look in the living room, and then – if there's what I'd call time, I'll run over and look in the bedroom. Worth a look.'

'Now, Hazel,' said Mum. 'In you go.'

And Mum put Hazel safely back inside the hutch.

First Hazel looked at her bowl of dried food, and then she ran back into the bedroom to peep at the hay on the bedroom floor. Then she scuttled back into the living room to look for the bread and carrots. And then she paused. Had she really seen what she thought she had seen in the bedroom? She thought that she had seen a handsome black, white, and orange boy guinea pig, the colour of tobacco.

She turned. She chirruped. That *was* what she had seen! She went back into the bedroom and burrowed in the hay.

The new guinea pig was called Tobacco.
They made a very happy pair.

The Visit of Fudge

The new guinea pig was called Tobacco. He had a contented nature, he enjoyed his food and he liked Hazel. They made a very happy pair. Hazel lost that slight wistfulness which she had had when she lived on her own. She no longer scurried about so much, everlastingly on the lookout for something. She had found what she was looking for. She discovered that many of life's simple pleasures were twice as enjoyable when they were shared with an amiable companion. In the old days, if someone had put an apple core in the hutch, she would have eaten it cheerfully enough. But now, as well as there being something to eat there was something to talk about.

'Anything important?' Tobacco called from the bedroom, hearing that there had been a delivery next door.

'A bit of fruit, by the looks of things,' said Hazel.

'Fruit, eh?'

Hazel never fully remembered *all* the fruits that there were, but Tobacco had a real knowledge of the subject. As he came out of the bedroom he said, 'It could be a piece of orange peel. Then again, it could be a pear.'

'Ar,' said Hazel. 'It could be a pear.'

She was eating some of it and couldn't rightly make up her mind.

'It could be, girl,' Tobacco conceded.

He had taken to calling Hazel 'girl,' and she seemed to like it, though she never called him 'boy'.

'But as it happens, this is ...'

'It's nice,' said Hazel.

'That it is,' said Tobacco, sinking his teeth into the apple core. He had momentarily forgotten what this particular fruit was called, but it was very delicious.

When they had nibbled it down to almost nothing, Tobacco shared with Hazel some of his almost-memories of the old days. He had no memory for things that had happened very recently. But there were some fascinating things lodged in his memory from three or four weeks before, when he lived with his parents in a rather over-crowded hutch. He did not *know* that they had been his parents, and when he thought of his father, it was simply a half-memory of an old black and white guinea pig who had talked rather a lot.

'I knew a guinea pig once...' said Tobacco, remembering his father but not *knowing* that it was his father.

'Now I can't remember whether I ever did,' said Hazel.

'This guinea pig,' said Tobacco, 'he said the best fruit to eat was called the Barn Anna. White, I believe it is.'

'More like a cabbage?' asked Hazel.

'Could be.'

'This here fruit was nice,' said Hazel, surveying the few remnants of the apple core. 'What did you say it was? My memory's terrible. Not like yours.'

Tobacco went to the bars of the hutch and sniffed.

'It's a really nice day today, girl. Let's hope they put us out on the lawn.'

A few minutes later the children came and put the guinea pigs in the run on the lawn. When Tobacco and Hazel ran about together on the grass, they were a joy to see. They were so happy, so playful, so carefree.

Now it so happened that on that day, the children who looked after the guinea pigs were planning a surprise for Tobacco. The girl had told all her school friends about him. Yes, Hazel was a wonderful, beautiful creature. And when she had owned just Hazel, the girl had believed that it would not have been possible to love a guinea pig more. But after Tobacco arrived, well…comparisons are odious. The girl did love Tobacco very, very much indeed. He was so friendly and happy, and he chirruped when you picked him up and put him in your jumper. The girl had told her friends that Tobacco was the handsomest, the most chirruping, the friendliest, and the best *boy* guinea pig in the world.

The girl's best friend, another girl called Rona, was also very fond of guinea pigs, and she had one whom she considered the prettiest, the most chirruping, et cetera: Fudge was a special breed, known by guinea pig experts (or, as they call themselves, Cavy fanciers) as American Crested.

The girl who looked after Hazel and Tobacco knew that no girl guinea pig could be nicer than Hazel. But she agreed with Rona that it would be very exciting if Fudge could have some babies. And if the prettiest, most chirruping, et cetera were to mate with the handsomest, most chirruping, et cetera, they would have the most et cetera *baby* guinea pigs in the world. Some of them might even turn out to be et cetera *cresteds*, and that was an exciting thought. So the girl had agreed that Rona should bring round Fudge that Saturday morning, and that Fudge should spend the weekend in a separate hutch with Tobacco. But as with so many things that sound like a good idea, it actually turned out badly.

'This,' Tobacco was saying, 'is what I'd call juicy. Really juicy grass, this.'

Hazel gazed at him admiringly. He had such a way of putting things. But just then the side of the run was lifted up, and a hand reached in and grabbed Tobacco in mid-sentence. He was just saying, 'I know this guinea pig once who knew about grass...'

'Don't squeak, Baccy darling,' said the girl. 'You are going to meet Fudge.'

'Oh, he *is* sweet,' said Rona. 'He's so nice and glossy.'

'Fudge is nice, too,' said the girl politely.

Tobacco stayed still in the girl's hands and quietened down. She sat on the grass and held him in her lap. He looked this way and that. This way he could see the wife, running about the run, saying, 'Ar, juicy, that's the word for it.' And that way, the other way, he could see some knees, clad in a pair of jeans, and some hands on which the nails were rather bitten down, and in the hands the silliest-

*It was the silliest-looking guinea pig
Tobacco had ever seen in his life.*

looking guinea pig Tobacco had ever seen in his life. It was an orange affair (not that he troubled himself about colours; as it happened he couldn't make out colours). And it had this sort of fur-hat thing on its head. Well, really! Tobacco tried to think of a word for it and selected the word *silly*.

'I mean,' he said quietly to himself, 'a head's a head. Just a head. You don't need to go dolling it up with a sort of *hat* effort.'

'I think he chirruped then,' said the girl optimistically.

'It sounded more like a whimper,' said her friend Rona.

'No,' said the girl firmly, 'it was a definite chirrup.'

'I so very much hope,' said Rona, 'that they'll like one another.'

'It is impossible not to like Tobacco,' said the girl.

'Shall we try putting them together in the hutch?' said Rona.

The girl stood up and carried Tobacco down to the garden shed where the hutches were, and Rona followed carrying Fudge. The girl opened the bedroom door of the hutch and put Tobacco inside. Tobacco felt disappointed that he had been given such a very *short* time in the run. He had been enjoying the fresh air, and the grass, and the good talk. But he contented himself with the certainty that Hazel would soon be brought to join him.

'Shall we put Fudge in the bedroom, too?' asked the girl.

'No,' said Rona, 'I'll put her in this living room part of the hutch.'

So this they did. And then they shut the doors, making sure that they were fastened securely. The two girls peered into the hutch. Fudge chirruped and nuzzled into Tobacco's feeding bowl.

'She loves that bran,' said Rona. Then she added coyly, 'I expect they want to be left on their own.'

And the two girls walked out of the shed, leaving the guinea pigs to their own devices. They went and sat on the lawn and watched Hazel munching her grass-feast in the run.

'Wouldn't it be lovely if Fudge had some babies?' said Rona.

'A whole litter of crested Tobaccos,' said her friend. 'As glossy and friendly and sweet as Tobacco, only with little crests on their heads! If Fudge *does* have a litter of babies, would you let me have one?'

'Would your mum let you have three guinea pigs?' asked Rona.

'Of course she wouldn't,' said the girl's brother, who had come out to join them. He thought it was soppy to be drooling over the little creatures in this way. He wanted someone to play tennis with and waved a racket grandly. 'Come and play a game.'

'Not if you're going to be rude about Baccy,' said his sister.

'I'd like to play,' said Roma.

So they all went to the nearby park to play tennis.

Inside the hutch, Tobacco lay in his hay bed for a while, and felt sad. Then he decided that there was no point in sulking, and he had no sooner made this sensible decision than his spirits lifted. He heard some munching and scuffling next door in the living room and he happily assumed that Hazel had been brought to join him.

'I could have done with longer on the grass, girl,' he called from the bedroom. But as he waddled out to join her, he did not hear the familiar cries of 'Ar' or 'That's right.' Instead, to his absolute amazement, he saw Silly Hat bold as brass, standing in *their* living room and eating *their* food.

'Get back in there if you value your life,' said Fudge angrily.

'What did you say?'

'You heard.'

'That's not manners,' said Tobacco. 'And who are you, I would like to know.'

As he spoke, all the fur stood up on his back. He felt a violent hostility to Silly Hat. He felt so angry that he would have liked to bite the silly pig.

'Warned you!' said Fudge, who ran towards Tobacco with fur on edge and teeth bared.

The fight was sharp and furious. Fudge tried to jump on Tobacco's back and bite his neck. Tobacco threw Fudge off and scratched at the enemy with his claws. Then to his great satisfaction, he managed to get a good mouthful of Fudge's crest. He yanked and tugged with his teeth and succeeded in pulling

Fudge tried to jump on Tobacco's back and bite his neck.

out some of the fur before Fudge hit him with a claw on the side of his head and knocked him dizzy.

'I'll teach you to pull my crown, you common little *brat*!' howled Fudge.

'Crown! Huh! Silly hat more like,' said Tobacco.

He regretted saying this, because it excited in Fudge a truly murderous fury.

'No one insults the cresteds and gets away with it,' hissed Fudge through two slightly protuberant front teeth, both very sharp. 'Particularly not a *thing* like you.'

Fudge pounced on poor Tobacco and knocked him over on his back. Tobacco waved his paws and shrieked in despair; he was completely powerless. He looked up and saw the open mouth of Fudge and two long sharp fangs coming closer and closer to his throat.

She stroked him, kissed him and examined his cut.

Then, just in the nick of time, the door of the hutch opened, and Mum's hand reached inside and picked up Tobacco. He was quivering with fright, and he had a cut on the side of his head.

'Poor Tobacco,' said Mum.

She stroked him, and kissed him, and examined his cut. It was not as bad as it looked. Mum put Tobacco in the run with Hazel. Then Mum went to the garden shed once more. She took Fudge out of Tobacco and Hazel's hutch.

'Come on, Fudge,' said Mum. 'We'll put you in this spare hutch over here.'

It just happened that Mum had been weeding the flower bed near the garden shed. She had heard the furious squeaking of Fudge and Tobacco and had gone to see what was the matter with them. Mum did not blame either of the guinea pigs for fighting. She was not cross with Fudge for having flown at Tobacco. She realised that it was just nature. She was just a *little* cross with the children for having gone off leaving the guinea pigs before checking that they were getting along well. A nasty incident had been narrowly avoided.

In the run Tobacco was still shaking with the shock of it all.

'How have you gone and got that nasty cut?' asked Hazel, her mouth full of grass.

'Silly Hat did it,' said Tobacco.

'What's that then?'

'You've been all right, girl, eating grass in here.'

'Ar,' agreed Hazel. 'I've been all right.'

'But they've gone and bought this terrible pig with a thing on its head like you've never seen.'

'What kind of a thing?'

'Well, hat's the only word for it,' said Tobacco. 'And a darned silly one at that.'

'Watch your language,' said Hazel.

'Well, silly, then, and never mind about the darned.'

'That's better.'

'And where do you think they've gone and put this Silly Hat creature?'

'Where?'

'In our hutch, that's where.'

'What, not in *our* hutch.'

'That's right, girl.'

'Another guinea pig?'

'Like I says, with this darned – sorry – with this Silly Hat thing on its head.'

'That wouldn't be right,' said Hazel. 'Not on its head, a hat.'

And then Tobacco felt fonder of Hazel than he had ever felt before, and he went and stood so that his nose was very nearly touching her nose. And then he thought how beautiful she was – so plump and sleek and brown and glossy. And he made a noise that the girl called chirruping – but actually he was saying, 'That's my girl.'

They talked for ages about Silly Hat while they munched their grass. Tobacco partly talked so much about it because he couldn't stop, and partly to remind himself of what had happened in case he forgot it.

'Then it came at me,' he said.

'Oh *dear*,' said Hazel.

'But I gave it what for,' said Tobacco.

'I bet you did,' said Hazel, 'but you shouldn't go fighting.'

Although Hazel said this, she was secretly very proud of Tobacco for defending their hutch against an intruder.

Tobacco said, 'Then I says, "Don't come a step further," I says, "or I won't be actionable for my answers."'

'Oh *dear*!' exclaimed Hazel.

'It came at me,' said Tobacco, 'but I were ready. Its teeth were bared, and it was hissing and oh, girl – the stink of the creature.'

'What did you do?' asked Hazel.

'Do?' asked Tobacco. 'What else could I do? I just fought it. I give as good as I got, girl.'

'I'm sure,' said Hazel. 'But you didn't ought to have got into no fight.'

'It come at me,' said Tobacco, 'but I knocked it sideways. Flat. That's what I knocked it. I really think if that lady hadn't come along, Silly Hat would have been a goner.'

'I'm glad you didn't…' Hazel hesitated. Either she could not find the word 'kill' or she did not want to use it. Instead she asked, 'Where are we going to live? We can't share a hutch with Silly Hat.'

'We shall *protest*,' said Tobacco. 'If they pick us up and tries to put us in that hutch with Silly Hat, we must wriggle, we must struggle, we must shout. We must never allow them to put us in there.'

When the children returned from their game, and tried to catch Tobacco and Hazel, they found it astonishingly difficult. Both the guinea pigs ran round the run and *wouldn't* be caught. And when they were eventually caught, they squealed and squealed, demanding to be free. But it was all right. When they got back to their hutch they found that Silly Hat had been taken away. She had gone home with Rona.

'I can still smell that *thing* in here, you know, girl,' said Tobacco, indignantly walking up and down the living room.

'Oh come to bed and stop worrying.'

Much later, as they lay in the hay, Tobacco said quietly to Hazel, 'I'm glad it's gone.'

'Me too,' said Hazel.

'I'm glad it's just you and me, girl.'

'That would be right,' said Hazel.

The whole incident caused the children embarrassment and worry. The girl had told Rona that Tobacco was so friendly. Rona had said the same thing about Fudge.

'And it would have been so wonderful if Fudge could have had Tobacco's babies,' said the girl.

'Wonderful, indeed,' said Mum. 'It would have been a miracle.'

'Why is that?' asked the girl.

'Surely you've realised by now,' said Mum, 'that Fudge is a boy.'

After a few weeks of living with Tobacco,
Hazel became even fatter.

Brown 'Un

Hazel was a very fat guinea pig. After a few weeks of living with Tobacco, however, she became even fatter. The children began to suspect that she was eating too much.

'It's like Mum and Dad,' said the boy. 'If Mum is on her own, she just eats a stick of celery and a tub of cottage cheese for her lunch. But when Dad's at home, she cooks a leg of lamb, roast potatoes, vegetables, pudding and custard.'

'Sometimes,' said the girl. 'Not always. Sometimes it's stew and dumplings, followed by rhubarb fool or ...'

'I know, I know,' said the boy. 'That was just

an example, stupid. Married people eat more than single people, it's a well-known fact.'

'How do *you* know?' asked his sister.

The boy did not bother to answer this question. He just said, 'It's the same with guinea pigs.'

'But Hazel doesn't give Tobacco his food,' said the girl. 'I'm the one who puts out the dried food and the raw carrots and the ...'

'When you remember,' said the boy. 'Usually it's Mum who feeds them.'

'It is not,' said the girl. 'Anyway, you may be right. I shall try giving them less to eat in the future.'

So that day she only half filled the guinea pigs' bowl with bran and instead of giving them one raw carrot each, she cut a carrot in two and put that in their cage.

Hazel and Tobacco did not notice that their rations had been halved when the food arrived.

'Grub's up,' squeaked Tobacco.

'Eh?'

'Wonder what it'll be today. Now I feel like a nice carrot.'

'Carrots? Oh good.'

And Hazel scuttled into the living room part of their cage and started to nibble her half carrot. She found her meal very delicious. But when she had eaten her carrot and rummaged about in the blue plastic food bowl, she felt her meal had been strangely unsustaining. Tobacco felt the same.

'I'll be glad when we're out on the lawn,' said Hazel.

'Same here,' said Tobacco. 'I could just do with a few mouthfuls of grass. Just to round off the meal nicely.'

But that day it was raining, and the children did not put the guinea pigs out in the run. After about an hour and a half they were squeaking with hunger.

This went on for two or three days. The little girl gave the guinea pigs smaller meals, and they both felt acutely hungry and miserable. And there was this curious fact. In spite of her special diet, Hazel remained decidedly stout. In fact, the less she ate, the fatter she became.

Then the girl had a horrible thought. She had several times seen films and pictures of very hungry people in Africa, and she remembered that when poor children are dying of starvation, their stomachs swell up. Perhaps the reason that Hazel was getting fatter and fatter was that she was starving.

'Don't be stupid,' said her brother. 'How can she be starving? And anyway, that doesn't explain why she is so *much* fatter than Tobacco.'

So they decided to ask Mum why Hazel was getting so fat, but Mum just smiled and said, 'Wait and see.'

Mum also told the girl to go on feeding Hazel and Tobacco a normal amount of food. She also said that it would be better, even though the sun was now shining, if Hazel did not go out in the run. Tobacco could go in the run but not Hazel.

'I expect you can guess why Hazel wants to be a bit quieter,' said Mum.

'She doesn't like the hot weather,' said the boy. 'That's why.'

But the girl had by now guessed the real reason that Hazel had become so very, very fat. She took special care to clean out the hutch every day. She made sure that Hazel had plenty of clean hay in the bedroom. And she gave her *extra* little bowls of bread and milk to eat.

'It's not just herself that she has to feed, is it, Mum?' said the girl. But the boy just looked puzzled. And sure enough, after not many days, the girl's expectations were fulfilled.

And she gave her extra little bowls of bread and milk to eat.

It happened early one morning before the people in the house were up. Tobacco and Hazel were in the hutch. It was a bright sunny morning and outside the birds were singing. Tobacco had woken early, thinking of his breakfast.

'Hazel,' he said, 'if someone was to come along and offer me a cabbage stalk, I shouldn't say no.'

'I should,' said Hazel.

Early in the morning, a guinea pig does not always listen to what his wife is saying, so Tobacco continued, 'Or a nice bit of lettuce. I shouldn't say no to a nice bit of lettuce.'

'Don't feel like eating,' said Hazel.

'What's that?'

'It's all right,' said Hazel. 'Just don't feel too like my food, that's all.'

'Are you all right, girl?' asked Tobacco, suddenly anxious for Hazel's welfare.

'Oh, I'm all *right*,' said Hazel. 'Just got a *twinge*, that's all.'

'A twinge, eh? What sort of a twinge? A twinge of hunger?'

'More like just a twinge,' said Hazel. 'A twinge inside, like.'

'You'll be better when you've got a drop of grub inside you,' said Tobacco.

'All the same,' said Hazel, 'think I'll just go into the bedroom. Have a lie down in the hay.'

An hour later Mum brought Tobacco his breakfast, and after she had put some bran in his bowl and some lettuce leaves on the living room floor, she opened the bedroom door and peered into the hay. Then Mum called, 'Children! Children! Come and see!'

Tobacco had been thinking that his wife was being a long time in the bedroom. He wondered what all the excitement was about and between mouthfuls of a really delicious piece of lettuce he called through, 'Everything all right, dear?'

'I think so,' Hazel called back.

'Grub's up,' said Tobacco.

'Ar.'

But she did not come. So Tobacco pushed his nose into the bedroom. And there he saw Hazel and three bedraggled little guinea pigs lying beside her in the hay.

'Now how did *those* get in there?' was Tobacco's first thought. And then he realised what had happened. He knew why Hazel was so quiet that morning. He stared at the mystery of it. Half an hour before, Hazel had just been an overweight guinea pig. And now – here were three *new* guinea pigs. He knew where they had come from, but even so it felt like magic. And the magic feeling made him both sad and happy at once.

*And there he saw Hazel and three bedraggled little
guinea pigs beside her.*

By then Mum and the little girl were opening the bedroom door and peering inside.

'Don't touch them,' said Mum. 'Just look.'

'Oh, look!' said the girl. 'She's going to feed them.'

The little guinea pigs, who still looked rather bedraggled and surprised to be existing at all, were beginning to cluster around their mother for some milk.

'Are you all right, dear?' asked Tobacco.

'Yes,' said Hazel.

'Oh listen, they're *squeaking*,' said the girl.

'Squeaking or speaking,' said Mum.

And then, instead of feeding the babies all at once, Hazel lay down and … had another baby!

It was a very small baby, not much bigger than a mouse, and for a while it lay perfectly still. Mum and the little girl and Tobacco all watched, and they all feared the worst. But the baby was not dead.

Hazel was a good mother. She cleaned it up, and she licked it, and she petted it, and soon the tiny, mouse-like little guinea pig was staggering about with the others.

'That all?' asked Tobacco. Naturally he was proud and pleased to be a father, but enough is enough.

'I *think* so,' said Hazel.

And before long the four babies had all been suckled, and were lying contentedly against their mother's soft, furry body.

There was no room for all six of them in one hutch. Mum insisted after this that Tobacco be moved into a separate hutch, which made him very desolate and lonely. His hutch was at right angles to Hazel's, so they could see each other through the wire. Every morning he would call out, 'All right, girl?' And Hazel would reply, 'Right you are.' Each evening Tobacco would say, 'Sleep well, girl!' and Hazel would say, 'Right you are.' But all through the day and night, he was lonely without her. She was not so lonely without him. She had four other guinea pigs for company and found it an exhausting occupation keeping them fed and trying to teach them some manners.

The guinea pigs themselves did not know about Mum's decree. Mum had decreed that two guinea pigs were enough and, rather meanly, Dad and the boy had agreed with her. It had been further decreed that when the guinea pigs were four weeks old, they should be taken to the pet shop. This was only sensible.

'So you must not get too fond of them,' said Mum to the little girl. 'There really is no point.'

Of course there is no *point* in getting fond of anything. It was easy to say that they should not get fond of the guinea pigs. But if you were seeing them every day, as the little girl was, you couldn't *help* getting fond of them.

So it was agreed that the babies of Hazel and Tobacco should be called One, Two, Three, and Four. 'One' was a cheeky, rather brash guinea pig, nearly all white with a few brown patches on his back. He was the first who started to eat solids, and he strutted about the cage as if he owned it. 'Two' was a tortoiseshell and white male, slightly more mysterious in character. He was very fond of his food and kept himself to himself.

'Three' was an amiably stupid brown and white female who very early on took to imitating her mother's phrases. But she never knew the meaning of them. If Hazel called out, 'Come and have some milk!', 'Three' would rush into the bedroom saying, 'That would be right.' If Hazel licked 'Three' behind the ears and said, 'Why can't you be *neat*?', 'Three' would answer, 'Right you are.' And when she was settling down to sleep in the hay, very sleepy with her eyes shut, 'Three' sometimes murmured, 'Wouldn't mind a nice run on the lawn.'

So much for the guinea pigs known as 'One', 'Two', and 'Three'.

But 'Four' was the little girl's favourite. She liked 'Four' because she was small and brown and vulnerable. She liked 'Four' because she chirruped when you picked her up. She liked 'Four' because she was the baby of the family. Most of all she liked 'Four' because she was 'Four'. In fact the girl liked 'Four' so much that she secretly called her by her proper name. When she was alone by the hutch, the girl would say, 'Hello One! Hello Two! Hello Three!' to the first guinea pig babies. But when 'Four' appeared, looking round to make sure that no one was near, the girl whispered, 'Hello, Beryl!'

They took the guinea pigs to the pet shop in a basket and showed them to the pet shop man.

So of course Mum was right, and there was no point in getting fond of them. But by the end of the month the girl was very fond of the baby guinea pigs, especially of Beryl.

It had been agreed that the girl should go with Mum when she took the little pigs to the pet shop.

'I bet you blub,' said the boy.

'I shan't,' said the girl. And she had really made up her mind that however sad she felt in the pet shop, she was not going to cry.

They took the guinea pigs to the pet shop in a basket which they showed to the pet shop man.

'Oh!' he said. 'They *have* been well looked after.' And he got them out of the basket, One, Two and Three.

'Just three is it? They all seem fine healthy specimens.'

'No,' said Mum, 'there are four. There's another one down in the hay.'

'So there is,' said the man, lifting out Beryl. 'She's not such a fine specimen as the others, is she?'

'She was born last,' said Mum.

'That would account for it,' said the man. But to the girl at that moment it seemed perfectly obvious that Beryl was the most beautiful guinea pig in the world.

'Right-ho!,' said the man. 'I don't know if I can sell this last one – but the other three, I could give you one pound each.'

And the girl thought, 'Oh *good*, I shall be able to keep Beryl after all.'

But Mum said, 'Please take all four. We simply don't have room for the last one – if you didn't like it, I'm afraid we should …'

The girl looked despondently at Mum. What *did* she mean? There would be *plenty* of room in the two hutches for just one extra guinea pig.

'Oh, all right,' said the man. 'But I can give you

only fifty pence for the little one. She *is* the runt of the litter.'

The man put the little pigs into a cardboard box and oh! how they squeaked. Seeing the girl's face become anxious the man said, 'I'm just putting them in here until I've got the window ready.'

And then Mum and the girl went home, saying goodbye to the pigs in the shop. The girl had been very good and not cried. Walking home, the girl was also very good and didn't cry. But when she got home, she ran down to the hutches to talk to Tobacco and Hazel, and there she did cry – quietly, but for a long time.

Guinea pigs have shorter memories than we do. About ten minutes after the little pigs had gone to the pet shop, Tobacco called across from his cage to Hazel's, 'Everything all right?'

And she had replied, 'Right you are.'

'Kids all right?' he'd asked.

 71

Now *kids*. Hazel knew there had been something on her mind. She had run into the living room to get them, and at that moment she had got distracted. A bowl of bread and milk it was that distracted her. And by the time she had eaten her fill, she had forgotten that she was looking for her children. Tobacco's question reminded her.

'Don't know where they've got to,' she called back.

'They'll be in the run – that's it,' said Tobacco. 'Out on the lawn.'

By the time the girl came to commiserate with the grieving parents, both Hazel and Tobacco had more or less forgotten that they had ever *had* any children.

'Are you sad, darling Hazel?' asked the girl through her tears.

But Hazel called back politely, 'Thank you for the bread and milk, ma'am. Very tasty.'

'That's right,' joined in Tobacco. 'A very tasty piece of bread you give me over here and all.'

'Oh listen *how* they are squeaking and missing their babies,' said the girl.

Mum had come to join her.

'They'll be all right,' said Mum. 'They'll get over it.'

'If you could ever manage to get us a *parsnip*,' called Tobacco. 'Now speaking for myself – I very much like parsnip.'

'Oh it is *sad*,' said Mum. 'I think he really does miss the little ones.'

The girl slept, but she woke every early the next morning. She knew as soon as she woke up that there was something to be sad about but, at first, she could not remember what it was. And then the memory of yesterday returned with dreadful force, and she thought of the baby guinea pigs, squeaking in that box in the pet shop. She got up and put on her red flannel dressing gown and went downstairs and opened the back door. Outside in the garden the weather was sunny and cheerful. The birds were singing in the eaves of the house and in the forsythia bush. And somehow the fact that the world of nature looked and sounded so cheerful made the girl all the sadder. She went to the garden shed and opened the door.

'Sounds like breakfast,' called Tobacco.

'Eh?' shouted Hazel from her hutch to his. 'Breakfast, eh?'

'You *poor* things,' said the girl when she heard their piping voices. But she had not brought their breakfast, which made them squeak all the more. In the event, she opened Tobacco's hutch and took him back upstairs to her bedroom. She got back into bed and gave him a celery stick which she had had the foresight to procure from the refrigerator on the way.

It was Saturday. The family had had their breakfast. Dad and the boy packed a basket and said that they were going out fishing. Mum said that she was going shopping, and when she had given the girl her pocket money, the girl said she would like to come to the shops with Mum. First they went to the grocer's and bought butter, biscuits, drinking chocolate, and cheese. Then they went to the butcher and bought a chicken and a pound of sausages. Then they went to the baker and bought a white loaf, a brown loaf, four tea-cakes, and two gingerbread men. And then they went to Mum's favourite café, and Mum had a cup of coffee, and the girl had a milkshake. Now all these shops and the café were in the covered market in the centre of the town, in the very place where the pet shop was. It took the girl only two minutes to drink her milkshake through a straw, but Mum was lingering, in the annoying way that grown-ups

'Mam – get us a gerbil,' said a little boy.
'You shut up,' said his mother rudely.

do linger over their drinks. She had hardly started her coffee.

'Mum,' said the girl, 'would it be all right if I went out and looked at a few shop windows? I won't go far.'

'Provided you don't leave the covered market,' said Mum, 'and provided you don't talk to strangers, and provided you are only five minutes.'

So the little girl left the café and walked to the next aisle of the market. And there on the corner was the pet shop window. There was a little group of people staring in at the window. Some were looking at a green lizard in a tank; and some were looking at the goldfish. But the greater part of them were looking at a lower window that contained... Beryl! There was Beryl, all on her own, nibbling some bran from a bowl and looking nonplussed by all this attention.

Evidently the other three babies had already

been sold and, to judge from the talk at the window, Beryl would soon be sold too.

'Mam – get us a gerbil,' said a little boy.

'You shut up,' said his mother rudely.

Another mother was saying, 'Isn't it sweet?'

'Can't we get it, Mummy, *please*?' said this other mother's daughter who looked – our girl considered – really horrible.

Our girl had only planned to have one last *look* at her guinea pig babies. She only wanted to see them, and to say goodbye. She really had not planned what happened next, but she found herself looking in her purse. Mum had let her keep half the money from yesterday's transaction, so she had £1.75. In addition, she had 50p pocket money from that morning and £1 in savings. Altogether she had £3.25. She had promised not to speak to strangers, but the man in the pet shop was not exactly a stranger. She found herself going into the shop. She felt very shy, and her heart was pounding excitedly.

The pet shop man took a long time before serving her. There were a lot of people in front of her, and every time they opened their mouths, the girl was afraid that they were going to ask if they could buy the guinea pig. But the man with the nobbly nose bought some dog food, and the short, fat woman with a scarf bought birdseed, and the two children bought hay … and at last it was the girl's turn.

'How much is the guinea pig in the window?' she blurted out shyly.

'At least you know what it is,' laughed the man. 'We had some people in just now thought it was a gerbil. It's four pounds. Very fine guinea pig. It's been beautifully reared.'

The man did not seem to recognise her as the girl who had sold him the guinea pigs the day before.

'You wouldn't take three pounds and twenty-five pence, I suppose,' said the girl.

'Well,' said the man. 'The price is …' He peered at her. Did he know? 'The price is really four pounds.'

'It is rather a small, puny guinea pig,' said the girl. 'Have you no others?'

'We had three others,' said the man, 'but they've all gone. Sold like hot cakes. And this,' he paused, 'this was the prize of the bunch.' He was obviously weakening because he then said, 'If you bought it, you would look after it properly wouldn't you? It's been beautifully handled and reared since birth, this cavy.'

'Oh, I would. I know how to look after guinea pigs. I have one or two already,' said the girl.

'Three is the ideal number to have,' said the man. 'Two females and one male. This one here's a female.'

The girl was clever. She did not say, 'I know.'
She said instead, 'You see, I only have three pounds
and twenty-five pence. I could let you have the other
seventy-five pence in a week's time.' And then the
man smiled and said, 'Oh, all *right*. You can have it
for three pounds and twenty-five pence.'

A few minutes later the girl reappeared at the
café, just as Mum was finishing her coffee. She was
carrying a little cardboard box, and out of it there
were coming the excited squeaks of Beryl.

'You needn't tell me what you've got in there,'
Mum said. 'I've guessed.'

'I wasn't planning to buy her, really, Mum, I
wasn't.'

'Which one is it?' asked Mum. 'I hope it *is* only
one? Three guinea pigs is quite enough.'

'It is Beryl,' said the girl.

'Not One, Two, Three or Four?'

'It is the one you call "Four,"' said the girl.

'You don't need to tell me what you've got in there,'
Mum said. 'I've guessed.'

'I shan't call her "Four" anymore,' said Mum. 'I shall call her Beryl. Beryl is a good name.'

About an hour later, Tobacco and Hazel were in their separate hutches.

'Coo-eee!'

'Is that you, girl?' asked Tobacco.

'No,' said Hazel, 'it wasn't me.'

'Thought I heard you call. Nice celery this morning, mine were.'

'I've tasted crispier,' said Hazel, 'but yes, it were nice.'

'Coo-eee!'

'There you go again,' said Tobacco.

'No I don't,' said Hazel. 'It's not me calling out. It's this new little brown 'un.'

'Brown 'un?'

'Yes,' said Hazel. 'When they come round with the celery this morning, they put this new brown 'un in to share with me.'

'Not a boar?' said Tobacco suspiciously.
'No, a little sow' said Hazel.

'Not a boar?' said Tobacco suspiciously. 'You're not sharing your cage with no he-pig?'

'No, a little sow,' said Hazel.

'That's all right then,' said Tobacco. 'Wonder why they didn't put her in to share with me?'

'She's nice,' shouted Hazel. 'More friendly to have someone to talk to.'

'Coo-eee!' shouted Beryl.

'Funny idea, bringing in another,' said Hazel, 'when we were all right on our own. But friendly, certainly.'

'Coo-eee, brown 'un!' shouted back Tobacco.

The End

Barn Anna Bread

'This guinea pig,' said Tobacco, 'he said the best fruit to eat was called the Barn Anna. White, I believe it is.'

Us humans like bananas to be a little bit more exciting. Here's a fun and easy recipe to make BANANAS into BREAD.

You will need:

- 220g self-raising flour
- 110g soft butter
- 200g soft brown sugar
- 4 medium-sized bananas (nice and brown)
- 2 eggs
- a pinch of salt
- 1tsp cinnamon, optional

1. Pre-heat the oven to 180°C and grease a loaf tin or small cake tin.

2. Mash the bananas with a fork and then mix with all the other ingredients until the flour has disappeared into the mixture.

3. Pour into the loaf tin.

4. Cook for about one hour or ask for help to test with a skewer/knife: if you poke it into the cake, and it comes out 'clean', your bread is cooked and ready to eat when it has cooled down!

Toilet Roll Tunnels

Hazel liked to explore. When she was in her hutch, she sometimes ran from one room to the next, as though she were looking for something.

Your guinea pig will love to explore, too. To make your pet a network of tunnels, you will need:

- Old kitchen rolls
- Scissors
- Old cardboard boxes.

Make sure your guinea pig can easily squeeze through a kitchen roll. Then, cut four 2cm slits into the end of the rolls. When they are cut, they will be able to squeeze together more easily to slip one inside the other.

Make two holes in a cardboard or shoe box and pop the rolls into the holes to create a fun den for your guinea pig. Experiment with hiding bits of food in places around the den so your pet can search for it.

Word Search

See if you can find all the words in the box.

M	P	G	W	D	B	E	R	Y	L
V	B	T	O	B	A	C	C	O	B
C	O	U	H	A	I	B	O	Y	A
A	O	G	A	B	U	P	L	B	N
B	T	R	Z	Y	I	X	Q	R	A
B	C	T	E	H	A	Z	D	N	N
A	M	G	L	P	A	P	S	T	A
G	U	P	I	F	L	D	P	D	I
E	M	I	C	R	D	F	M	L	F
E	J	G	C	J	L	C	V	D	E

BANANA   MUM

HAZEL   PIG

CABBAGE   GIRL

TOBACCO   BABY

APPLE   BOY

BERYL   BOOT

Match the Names

See if you can match the different guinea pig breed names to their pictures:

Short-haired

Abyssinian
(has rosettes on its coat)

Peruvian
(long-haired)

Silkie/Sheltie
(long hair going over body)

Rex

Teddy

Texel
(curly-haired)

Guinea Pig Facts

- Guinea pigs normally live for five to six years.
- Guinea pigs originally come from the Andes, in South America (the oldest recorded guinea pig was fourteen years, ten months and two weeks old).
- In the wild, guinea pigs live in groups of five to ten.
- A baby guinea pig can run when it is only three hours old!
- Young guinea pigs are known as pups, not piglets.

If you enjoyed Hazel's adventures, don't miss

Furball and the Mokes

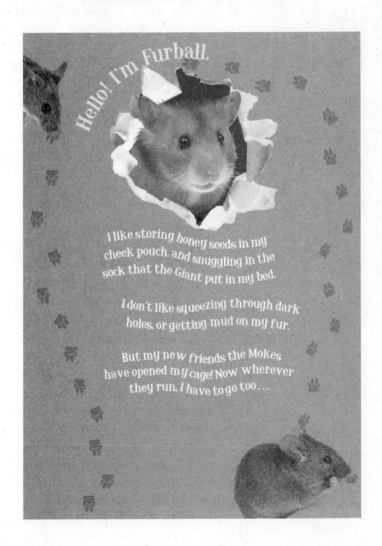

Hello! I'm Furball.

I like storing honey seeds in my cheek pouch, and snuggling in the sock that the Giant put in my bed.

I don't like squeezing through dark holes, or getting mud on my fur.

But my new friends the Mokes have opened my cage! Now wherever they run, I have to go too...